To: Maddie
From: Great Aunt Ryenee'
Easter 2006

D1530731

This is for you, Mom,
with love
~GH

This edition produced 2005 for
BOOKS ARE FUN LTD
1680 Hwy 1 North, Fairfield, Iowa, IA 52556

by LITTLE TIGER PRESS
An imprint of Magi Publications
1 The Coda Centre, 189 Munster Road, London SW6 6AW
www.littletigerpress.com

Originally published in Great Britain 2005
by Little Tiger Press, London
Text copyright © Jane Johnson 2004
Illustrations copyright © Gaby Hansen 2004

All rights reserved • ISBN 1 84506 178 0
Printed in China

10 9 8 7 6 5 4 3 2 1

Little Bunny's Bathtime!

Jane Johnson

illustrated by

Gaby Hansen

Little Tiger Press

"Bathtime for my bunnies!"
called Mrs. Rabbit, and her
children all came running.
All except her youngest
little bunny.

"I don't want a bath,"
said Little Bunny.
"I want to go on playing."

"You really want to play all by
yourself?" asked his mommy.
Little Bunny nodded, but
now he wasn't so sure.

"Well, you be good while
I'm busy with the others,"
said Mrs. Rabbit, plopping
them into the water.

"Swish, swash, swoosh," sang
the little rabbits happily, swirling
their bubbles around.

Little Bunny wanted
to play, too.

"Look at me!" he called,
hiding behind the towels.

"Yes, dear," said Mrs. Rabbit, but
she went on washing the others.
  "Tickly, wickly, wiggle toes," giggled
her little bunnies, wiggling their
feet in the water.

"Guess where I am?" shouted Little Bunny, hidden in the laundry basket.

"Found you," smiled his mother, lifting the lid . . .

But she turned back
to finish washing
the others.

"Up you come!" puffed Mrs. Rabbit,
lifting her children out of the tub.

"Rub-a-dub-dub, you've all had a scrub!"
she laughed. "What lovely clean
bunnies you are!"

Little Bunny was upset.
He wanted his mommy
to notice *him*.

So he
climbed
up . . .

and up—as far
as he could.
But suddenly . . .

... SPLASH!

He fell into the bathtub!

"Oh my!" said Mrs. Rabbit, fishing
him out right away.
    Little Bunny gazed up at her happily.
"I'm ready for my bath now, Mommy,"
he said, smiling sweetly.

Mrs. Rabbit couldn't help smiling back. "Off you go and play quietly," she said to the others.

Then she ran
fresh water and gave
Little Bunny a bath—
all to himself.

"Soapy ears and soapy toes,
soapy little bunny nose!" sang Mrs. Rabbit.
She washed his ears while he fluffed
up some new bubbles.
"I love you, Mommy," said Little Bunny.
"I love you too, darling."

She washed his back while
he played with his boat.
 "You're the best mommy in the
whole world," said Little Bunny.
 "And you're my precious
bunnykin."

She dried his fur
and whiskers, and said,
"Ooh, you smell
so clean and nice!"

And Little Bunny kissed his mommy
and hugged her tight.
"There now, all done," sighed Mrs. Rabbit.
"It's time for bed. Where are my other
little bunnies?"

She found them in the kitchen.
"Oh no! What a mess!" cried
Mrs. Rabbit. "You're dirty again!
You all need *another* bath!"

"Yes," giggled Little Bunny.
"All except me!"